For Heather, again

About this book

The illustrations for this book were created with digital collage, using original photos and textures arranged in Adobe Photoshop. Chamelia's and Cooper's outfits were inspired by fabrics generously provided by Alexander Henry Fabrics, Inc. (www.ahfabrics.com), and the cupcake images were used with permission of Blue Bird Bake Shop in Orlando, Florida (www.bluebirdbakeshop.com).

This book was edited by Connie Hsu and designed by Liz Casal
under the art direction of Patti Ann Harris. The production was supervised
by Charlotte Veaney, and the production editor was Christine Ma.
The text and display type are set in Barcelona.

Copyright © 2013 by Ethan Long

Little, Brown and Company * Hachette Book Group * 237 Park Avenue, New York, NY 10017 * Visit our website at www.lb-kids.com

Little, Brown and Company is a division of Hachette Book Group, Inc.
The Little, Brown name and logo are trademarks of Hachette Book Group, Inc.

The publisher is not responsible for websites (or their content) that are not owned by the publisher.

First Edition: July 2013

Library of Congress Cataloging-in-Publication Data * Long, Ethan. * Chamelia and the new kid in class / by Ethan Long.—1st ed. * p. cm. * Summary: Chamelia is used to being the star of her class, so when Cooper, a new student, becomes the center of attention, she is determined not to like him. * ISBN 978-0-316-21042-3 * (1. Popularity—Fiction. 2. Jealousy—Fiction. 3. Individuality—Fiction. 4. Chameleons—Fiction.) I. Title. * PZ7.L8453Chn 2013 * (E)—dc23 * 2012026497

10 9 8 7 6 5 4 3 2 1 * SC * Printed in China

Chamelia
and the New Kid in Class

by Ethan Long

Little, Brown and Company
New York   Boston

It was the first day of school, and Chamelia's friends
were excited to hear about her summer vacation.
Naturally, she chose to tell them through
song and dance.

Suddenly, her audience stopped watching.
"Children," said Mrs. Knight, "this is Cooper, your new classmate."
Everyone gathered around Cooper—everyone except for
Chamelia, who was just finishing Act One.

HI!

Cooper made friends fast.

In art class, all the kids wanted *him* to draw their portraits.

For the first time, no one paid any attention to *Chamelia's* works of art.

COOL!

During recess, Cooper won the game—and even more friends.

Chamelia was *not* used to losing.

After school, Cooper's new games were a hit,
but Chamelia didn't think they were special at all.

Besides, she had better things to do.

HMPH!

Cooper kept showing up wherever Chamelia went...even the supermarket!
He was seriously getting on her nerves.

When Cooper brought frosted cupcakes to school for his birthday, Chamelia was not impressed.

She bet they didn't even taste that good.

When Show-and-Tell Day came, it was time
to show everyone who the *real* star was.
Chamelia knew she had to be the best.

So Chamelia pulled out all the stops.

She danced.   She juggled.

She was a star!

Then it was Cooper's turn.

Even though Chamelia's shell collection was a hit,
Cooper's rocks looked really good, too.

He had to be stopped.

So she did all she could to distract him. She yawned.

She blew raspberries.

Her plan was working!

But as she watched Cooper, Chamelia got a heavy, horrible feeling
in her stomach.

Suddenly, being the best felt the worst.

So she decided to change her game plan and show the class
what it really meant to be a star.

You can do it, COOPER

As it turned out, Cooper's rock collection *was* really good.
So Chamelia cheered.

She applauded.

She was his biggest fan!

Chamelia could finally admit that the new kid was a star, too.

In fact, Cooper was supersweet!

That was all the more reason to make him a best friend...

...and an excellent sidekick!